"Let's get this Pilgrim party started!"

Little Patriot Press® is a registered trademark of Salem Communications Holding Corporation

Cataloging-in-Publication data on file with the Library of Congress
ISBN 978-1-62157-335-7

Published in the United States by
Little Patriot Press
An imprint of Regnery Publishing
A Division of Salem Media Group
300 New Jersey Ave NW
Washington, DC 20001
www.RegneryKids.com
www.Peanuts.com

Manufactured in the United States of America
10 9 8 7 6 5 4 3 2 1

Books are available in quantity for promotional or premium use. For information on discounts and terms, please visit our website: www.Regnery.com.

Distributed to the trade by
Perseus Distribution
250 West 57th Street
New York, NY 10107

It's a New World, Charlie Brown!

Peanuts created by Charles M. Schulz

Written by Tracy Stratford Illustrated by Tom Brannon

Little Patriot Press

"What did you pack in here?" Charlie Brown asked Sally. "Your backpack weighs a ton!"

"Just a few things for camp," Sally replied.

"Woo-hoo! Camp New World, here we come!" said Lucy. The kids were going on a field trip to see what life was like when the settlers came to America.

"You know things were different back then, right?" Charlie Brown asked. He was always worrying about his little sister.

"I'll be fine," Sally assured him. "As long as I get to watch TV."

The boys had big ideas for all the cool things they were going to do at Camp New World.

"I'm going to find a nice little pond and go fishing," Linus decided. Charlie Brown hoped to find a big bird like the one the Pilgrims caught.

Arriving at Camp New World, Lucy said, "I'm going to help the settlers with their style and fashion! Their clothes are so boring!"

"I want to play in the garden and pick pretty flowers," Sally said.

Peppermint Patty wanted to do a little candle making.

"Let's try pottery too!" Marcie said.

Everyone was excited to get started, but first, they had to change into colonial clothes. It took the girls a little longer. All those layers and so many buttons!

"Did someone forget to tell the settlers about jeans?"
Peppermint Patty asked. "How did they play baseball
in this getup?"

"Everyone ready to get this Pilgrim party started?" Franklin teased.

Linus said, "One of the first things they did was make an agreement to all work together. They called it the Mayflower Compact."

"Don't get Linus started on history stuff," Lucy groaned.

"That agreement sounds great," said Charlie Brown.
"One for all, and all for one!" they cheered.

Lucy walked into a building filled with flax, wool, and a spinning wheel. "Where are all the dresses?" she asked.

Sally found the garden. It was full of big orange pumpkins and all kinds of green vegetables. She also found lots of weeds to hoe, big baskets to fill, and plants to water.

Playing in the garden was a lot more work than Sally expected. Fortunately, a friendly neighbor stopped by to help. He was dressed differently, but he sure knew his way around the garden.

"Is that Squanto in the garden with Sally?" Linus was amazed. "The Pilgrims might have starved without his help growing crops."

Charlie Brown's big bird chase was on.

"What will you do if you catch it, Charlie Brown?"
Linus shouted.

"I'm not sure!" Charlie Brown yelled back.

GOBBLE, GOBBLE!

Meanwhile, the fish were jumping! If only Linus could figure out how to catch one. He only had a worm, a stick, a string, and a hook. His friends were counting on fresh fish for dinner.

Peppermint Patty had planned to make a nice candle for Marcie's birthday, but she found herself making many, many candles out of hot wax.

All the campers would be sitting in the dark tonight if she didn't make enough.

Marcie said, "No one told us that pilgrims had to make their own dishes! Thank goodness Squanto and the Wampanoags will share their pots with us!" Meanwhile, Franklin learned how to make soap.

First, he boiled ashes from a wood fire to get lye.

Then, he melted the fat he needed.

Next, he mixed and boiled the fat and the lye together

Finally, he poured the hot soap into wooden frames to cool and harden.

When Sally came in all dirty from the garden, Franklin offered her some of his new soap.

"Ugh!" Sally sniffed. "What is this stuff?"

"Ta-da! Let's get ready for the feast!"
Lucy announced as she spread a
very colorful cloth across the table.
Peppermint Patty's candles glowed, and
Marcie's pottery bowls were full of fruits
and vegetables from Sally's garden.

The fish Linus caught were on plates, and Franklin popped up popcorn to share.

"What a feast!" Sally said. "There's just one thing missing."

"Uh," Charlie Brown stammered. "About that big bird!"

"Let us all give thanks as the early settlers did!" Linus exclaimed.

"Bless this food and make us mindful of the needs of others. And...

"Thank goodness we survived!"

It's a New World

arly Settlers

ıe early settlers came from European countries such as
ain, England, Holland, and France, where good jobs
ere hard to find and land was expensive. By coming
America, many colonists hoped to have a better
ance at a decent living. In May 1607, 104 men
rived in Virginia to establish Jamestown, the
st permanent English settlement in North
nerica. The second English settlement was
arted by Pilgrims who arrived at Plymouth
ck, Massachusetts, in 1620 to escape religious
rsecution in Great Britain. They wanted the
portunity to worship freely.

ıe early years in Jamestown were difficult. In
e winter of 1608, a fire destroyed most of their
poden fort. Pocahontas, the daughter of the Indian chief
whatan, brought food and clothing to help the colonists. In
09, a drought destroyed the colonists' crops, causing starvation
d suffering. In 1612, Jamestown leader John Rolfe started growing tobacco in the colony.
hen other settlers saw his success, they started growing it too. Because tobacco could not
grown in England, English merchants began buying large quantities of tobacco from the
ttlers, and the Virginia Colony began to flourish.

mestown served as the capital of the colony for 83 years, from 1616 until 1699.

Massachusetts, the Pilgrims struggled to survive the winter of 1620—their first harsh
ew England winter. Nearly half of the Pilgrims died from starvation and disease. A Native
nerican named Squanto came to Plymouth and taught the survivors how to fertilize their
il and grow corn. Squanto also became their guide and translator (he spoke English!). That
lped the settlers communicate and get along better with the tribes that lived nearby.

s time passed, more and more ships arrived at Plymouth Colony, bringing additional settlers,
pplies, and livestock. In 1691, Plymouth became part of the Massachusetts Bay Colony.

Thanksgiving

The Pilgrims were not the first to celebrate Thanksgiving. Harvest celebrations and feasts to give thanks had been part of Native American tradition long before Europeans started coming to the New World. The Jamestown colonists also gathered for feasts of thanksgiving before the Pilgrims set foot on Plymouth Rock.

The early Thanksgiving celebrations sometimes lasted for days! Think about all the work that went into a Thanksgiving meal back then. Settlers had to grow and harvest their own fruits and vegetables or go out and pick them from wild plants. They hunted for their meat and fished for their seafood. They had to grind wheat and barley down to make flour for bread, then bake the bread in ovens. Whew!

When we think of Thanksgiving, we think of turkey, dressing, mashed potatoes, and apple pie. Those early settlers might have enjoyed eating turkey, but there were no mashed potatoes and no apple pie ... oh my! Potatoes and apples did not make their way to America until later.

What might have been on a table for a Pilgrim or Jamestown settler? Deer, turkey, fish, corn, beans, squash, pumpkins, wild onions, sweet potatoes, carrots, cabbage, lettuce, bread, acorns, walnuts, chestnuts, blueberries, strawberries, grapes, and gooseberries.

Pilgrims especially enjoyed cranberries and popcorn!